A Rather Remarkable Grizzly Bear

Marco
moves in

 GERRY BOLAND was born in Dublin but has lived in north Roscommon since 2001. He teaches creative writing in national schools in the area, works part-time in a local organic community garden, and spends as much time writing as he can. He is a committed environmentalist and an active campaigner on vegetarian and animal rights issues. His first collection of poems, *Watching Clouds*, was published by Doghouse Books in June 2011, and he is working on a collection of short stories. He is also the author of two travel books on Dublin.

Marco
moves in

Gerry Boland

Illustrated by Áine McGuinness

THE O'BRIEN PRESS
DUBLIN

First published 2011 by The O'Brien Press Ltd,
12 Terenure Road East, Rathgar, Dublin 6, Ireland.
Tel: +353 1 4923333; Fax: +353 1 4922777
E-mail: books@obrien.ie
Website: www.obrien.ie

ISBN: 978-1-84717-229-7

A catalogue record for this title is available from the British Library.

1 2 3 4 5 6 7 8 9
11 12 13 14 15

The O'Brien Press receives assistance from

Layout and design: The O'Brien Press Ltd
Cover illustrations: Áine McGuinness

Printed in the Czech Republic, in Finidr Ltd
The paper in this book is produced using pulp from managed forests

Dedication
to Saliman

Acknowledgements

Thanks are due to the following: The Tyrone Guthrie Centre in Annaghmakerrig; to Rena Dardis, for her encouragement and helpful comments early on; to the countless schoolchildren in counties Roscommon, Leitrim and Sligo who have been a consistent source of inspiration; to everyone at The O'Brien Press and to Mary Webb in particular; as always, to Miriam.

Marco
moves in

A grizzly bear walked all the way from the zoo to my front door and not a single person noticed him. I suppose it helped that it was night, and that he was wearing a big black duffle coat with an enormous hood that covered his hairy head. He knocked on the front door three times, loud knocks that shook the house.

'It'll be that grizzly bear that escaped from the zoo,' I said to my mum.

Mum was doing her breathing exercises for her trombone playing and she had her eyes closed. She didn't move from her armchair. Mostly, she just couldn't be bothered opening the door to visitors, leaving that important job to me.

'Quit your nonsense, Patrick,' she said. 'You know very well who it'll be: Sadie Sharp or Nosey Blunt.'

'It's the *grizzly*. It said on the news that he was seen in our neighbourhood.'

'Patrick, would you ever quit your nonsense,' she said again.

Mum says 'quit your nonsense' to me fifty times a day. I don't know why. I don't think I talk nonsense at all.

Now, to my surprise, she rose from her armchair and headed towards the hall.

I leapt up from the sofa and cut her off at the living room door.

'I'll get it,' I said. 'You go put the kettle on.'

Mum was good at doing lots of things, like playing the trombone at all hours of the day and night, but boiling the kettle and making tea was the thing she was best at. If there was a category in the Olympics for boiling kettles and making tea, Mum would have won the gold medal, no problem.

She walked down the hall, trombone across her shoulder, and disappeared into the kitchen, leaving me to open the door. Even though I'd guessed who it was, it was still a bit of a shock to see him standing in the porch. He was at least eight feet tall, and his fur was so wet he was dripping rain onto the ground.

'Any chance of a cup of tea?' he asked.

'You've come to the right house for that,' I said. 'Mum makes the best tea in Ireland.'

'So I heard,' he said. I knew by the way he licked his lips that he was desperate for a decent cup of tea.

'Come in,' I said.

Then I turned and walked back into the room. I heard the door close behind me and I heard his soggy feet making squelching sounds on the carpet as he followed me.

'Sit down and make yourself at home,' I said.

He stood in the doorway, his enormous body filling the space and blocking out the light from the hall. He stared at the TV. The ads were on.

'Were you watching the news?' he asked.

'I hate the news,' I said.

'There's a good chance I was on the news,' he said.

'That's pretty cool. Did you rob a bank, or what?'

Mum called out from the kitchen.

'Who was that at the door, Patrick?'

I didn't answer.

The grizzly shuffled into the room and sat
himself down on Mum's armchair.

'They call me Marco,' he said.

'Do you take milk and sugar, Marco?' I asked.

'Milk. No sugar. I'm trying to lose weight.'

I went to the doorway and called down the hall.

'Mum, our guest would like a pot of tea with milk and no sugar.'

'I suppose your mum will get a bit of a fright when she sees me sitting here in her living room?' the grizzly said.

'No need to worry about Mum. She's in a world of her own most of the time. Though she doesn't like anyone sitting in her armchair.'

Marco was obviously a bit of a wimp, for he shot out of the armchair and threw himself onto the sofa beside me. We must have looked an odd sight – the two of us sitting there on the sofa, watching TV.

'What's on the telly?' he asked.

Before I could answer, there was a gentle tap at the front door. I could feel Marco's body stiffen beside me. Another tap on the door, a little louder this time. Marco dived behind the sofa.

'What are you doing?' I laughed. 'It's only Mrs Sharp from next door. She calls every night to check if I got any supper.'

'Don't you usually?' he whispered from behind the sofa.

'Sometimes Mum forgets.'

Three more taps on the door.

'I'd better get it before she knocks any louder and brings Mum from the kitchen.'

'Will I stay here?'

'No. She'll spot you straight away. You're sticking out all over the place.'

'But what will Mrs Sharp say when she sees me?'

'Mrs Sharp is very nice, but she's a bit slow. Come out from behind the sofa and go over and stand in the corner. I'll say you're a hat-stand.'

I gently pushed him into a corner and helped him off with his coat.

I picked up an old gardening hat of Mum's that had been lying behind her armchair for ages and I put it on his head at an angle. As if someone had just flung it there.

Then I raised one arm and hung his coat over it.

'Don't move a muscle while she's here. She never stays very long.'

On the doorstep, Mrs Sharp was looking worried.

'You look as if you haven't eaten a thing all day, Patrick,' she said.

'I had a nice ripe banana and a lovely slice of toast,' I told her.

She pushed past me into the living room and stood gazing around her as if she didn't know where she was. She often looked like that.

'Well, I'm glad you got something, Patrick, but a slice of toast and a banana won't make you grow up into a big strong man.'

'What about gorillas?' I asked her.

'What about them?'

'They eat nothing but bananas and they're big
and strong. They don't even eat toast.'

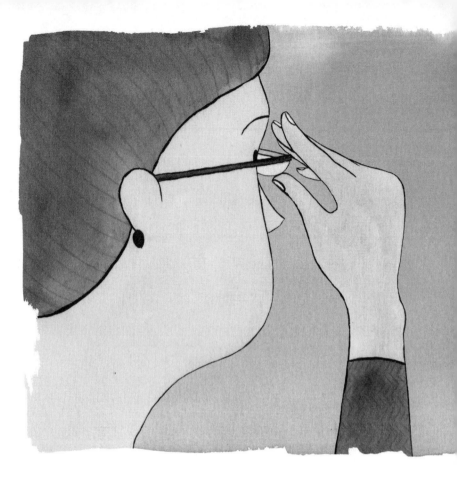

'What's *that*?' she asked suddenly, pointing to Marco.

'It's a hat-stand.'

'Strange place for a hat-stand. Where did it come from?'

'Mum picked it up for a song at the car boot sale.'

She took off her glasses, rubbed them on the sleeve of her cardigan and had another look.

'Good gracious, Patrick, it's a **grizzly bear!**'

'A *stuffed* grizzly bear, Mrs Sharp.'

'Poor grizzly. I don't think it's right to stuff animals. How would you like to be stuffed and used as a hat-stand?'

'I wouldn't be tall enough. Anyway, it's going back tomorrow. It's too big for the hall and a living room isn't the place for a hat-stand. People want to hang up their hats and their coats in the hall.'

She gave a heavy sigh and turned to leave.

'Is your mother in the garage?'

'Where else?'

'What's she working on today?'

'She's making a hat-stand in the shape of a grizzly bear. One that will fit in the hall.'

I had long ago learned that Mrs Sharp would believe anything I told her. I told her lots of crazy things. And she never once told me 'quit your nonsense'.

Marco was sitting on the sofa when I came back in. One arm was sticking out, the other was up in the air.

'You were **terrific**,' I said. 'You didn't move a muscle. Mrs Sharp really thought you were a hat-stand.'

'Mrs Sharp is obviously a bit mad in the head. And my arm is about to fall off.'

'Don't be silly, arms don't fall off.'

'If you hold up your arm long enough, the blood drains away and it withers and falls off.'

'That's just an old grizzly tale. Take your arm down and move it around a bit and it will be fine.'

'Is your mum really out in the garage? I thought she was making us tea.'

I said nothing. I liked having fun with Mrs Sharp, but I didn't want to tell Marco that Mum spent most of her time doing pretty unusual things.

Like playing the trombone.

Or the drums.

Or chiseling enormous boulders for weeks and weeks in the garage, until one day, instead of a giant boulder, there would be a huge stone head of a giraffe.

No one at school had a mum like my mum. Not even near.

'She's taking an awful long time,' Marco said. 'I'm parched.'

I left him sitting where he was and I went to get the tea. I could hear Mum playing her trombone in the garage. She had made the tea. The pot and the cups and the milk jug, as well as a plate of chocolate biscuits, were placed neatly on our good tray. I picked it up and carried it slowly and carefully to the living room.

Just as I was putting the tray on the coffee table, there was another knock on the door.

'Is that Mrs Sharp coming back to check on you again?' Marco asked.

'No. It'll be Mr Blunt. Mrs Sharp lives on one side of us and Mr Blunt lives on the other.'

'Is he checking up on you, too?'

'Yep. He always checks to see if I've done my homework.'

'Does your dad not do that?'

'Dad isn't here. He went off somewhere and hasn't come back. Mr Blunt is pretending to be a kind of dad, but to tell you the truth, he isn't very good at it.'

There was another knock on the door.

'It's best if he doesn't find you here. He doesn't like animals, especially gigantic ones like you.'

'I'm **NOT** going to be a hat-stand again!'

'Lie down on the floor. I'll say you're a bearskin rug.'

'That'll never work. If I was a rug, I'd be flat and you could walk on me.'

'I'll say you're a secondhand rug that got some air trapped in it and we picked it up for …'

'I know … a song.'

'Exactly. Go on, quick, lie down there in front of the TV. I'll turn off the main light so he won't be able to see properly.'

'It's very dark in here,' said Mr Blunt when he came in.

'We're saving energy. To help slow down global warming.'

He headed towards the armchair but tripped over a stool and fell flat on his face. His left eye was only inches from Marco's right eye.

'**What on earth is that?**' he asked.

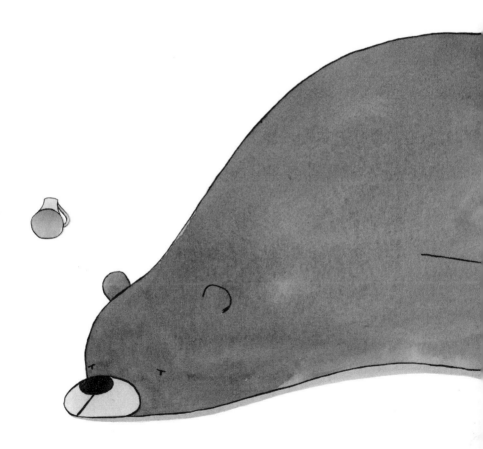

'It's a bearskin rug.'

'What a disgusting object! I hate any rug made from an animal. And I especially hate bears. Yuk!'

He picked himself off the floor and wiped himself down.

'Well, son, did you get your homework done?'

'Yes Mr Blunt. All done.'

He peered down at Marco.

'That's a very poor quality rug you have there. Even in the bad light I can tell it came from a half-starved, very ugly bear. And what a pong! How can you stick the smell?'

I was afraid that Marco would either burst out crying or that he'd get up and throw Mr Blunt out the window so I said the first thing that came into my head. Luckily, it was quite a sensible suggestion.

'I'm off to bed. I've an early start in the morning.'

'You stay up far too late, son,' Mr Blunt said, heading for the back door, his left hand covering his nose. 'I'll have to have a word with your mother. A boy of your age should be in bed by nine.'

'Mum went to bed early.'

'I thought I heard her playing the trombone in the garage.'

'That's Mrs Sharp. She's trying it out before she goes ahead and buys one.'

That stopped him in his tracks. Mr Blunt wasn't a big fan of Sadie Sharp's. He turned around.

'I'm off, son. I can't keep up with the comings and goings around here. Get a good night's sleep.'

'I will. Bye.'

When I got back, Marco was brushing his coat.

'Mr Blunt is *very* blunt,' he said. 'Do I really smell that bad?'

'Don't worry about it. Everyone has their own smell. I have mine, and you have yours. Yours might be a little stronger than mine, but that's ok. In any case, Mum has no sense of smell, so she won't even notice.'

All this time, the tea was sitting in the pot, waiting patiently to be poured.

'Will we have our tea now?' I asked.

He looked at the teapot, the jug of milk, the plate of biscuits. His eyes widened and he smiled his first smile of the evening.

'Is that what I think it is?' he asked, staring at the pot.

'Sure is. Will I pour?'

'Please.'

He sat down beside me on the sofa, but before I could pour a drop there was a loud knock on the door.

'Mr Blunt again?' said Marco. 'Mrs Sharp? Or do all your neighbours drop in every night?'

This time I couldn't tell who was at the door. But it was a *really* loud knock and I suspected that whoever was there would probably want to come in.

I picked up the tray and told Marco to put the coffee table into the corner where he had been a hat-stand earlier. Then I told him to get down on all fours where the coffee table had been. I told him to arch his back so that it was really straight and not to dare move a muscle.

Then I placed the tray gently on his back. It didn't even wobble.

'Ok, that looks good. You're a coffee table. Hopefully, you won't be needed.'

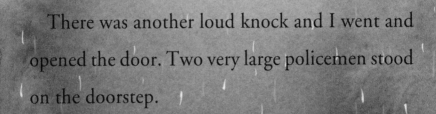

There was another loud knock and I went and
opened the door. Two very large policemen stood
on the doorstep.

'A grizzly bear has escaped from the zoo. We're carrying out a house-to-house search. Mind if we have a look inside?' one of the policemen said.

They looked fed up to be out and about on such a cold and wet night. A thought flashed into my head: I might be arrested!

'Why would a grizzly bear hide in our house?' I asked.

'We get to ask the questions, young man. I'm Sergeant Calloway and this is Constable Strummer. Now, how about letting us in?' said the smaller of the two policemen.

They followed me in to the living room.
Sergeant Calloway stared at the teapot and the
biscuits and licked his lips, just like Marco had
done earlier. There was nothing for it but to offer
them a cup of tea.

'Milk?' I asked as I poured.

'Please,' came the reply from both.

'Sugar?'

'Two spoons.'

'Three for me.'

There was no sugar on the tray so I had to leave
Marco and the two policemen in the living room
on their own while I went to get some from the
kitchen. When I returned, they were both sitting
on the sofa, eating the chocolate biscuits. I put
sugar in their tea, stirred both cups, then went
and sat in Mum's armchair.

'Where are your parents?' Sergeant Calloway asked.

'They're playing in a jazz band down at the Coliseum. They won't be back till late.'

'You're in the house on your own?'

'Me and the grizzly bear.'

They both nearly choked on their tea.

'Just joking,' I said.

'Funny man,' Sergeant Calloway said. 'Come on, John, let's leave this comedian and find our grizzly bear.'

As they went out through the front door, the young policeman gave me a smile and said 'thanks', but Sergeant Calloway didn't say a word.

Marco was still a coffee table when I returned. I took the tray off his back.

'Up you get. Put the coffee table back where it was and sit down and relax. I won't be long.'

A few minutes later, we were once again sitting on the sofa. The tray was on the table, there was a new batch of chocolate biscuits on the plate, and a pot of freshly brewed tea. Marco watched as I filled his cup and added a little milk.

'Lovely job, Patrick,' he said, taking the cup in his beautiful bear hands. He brought the cup to his lips and took a careful sip.

'Your mum has taught you how to make a nice pot of tea.'

'I'm a good learner,' I said.

Marco took another few sips, then looked me straight in the eye.

'Poor you. You don't get a chance, do you?'

'I get by.'

'Why don't you and I run away?'

'Where would we go?'

'Anywhere we wanted. Maybe to where my family come from.'

'Where's that?'

'The Rocky Mountains.'

'Wouldn't it be freezing up in the Rockies?'

'It would be a bit cold alright. But we could take shelter in the forests.'

'We have trees here,' I said. 'At the end of the garden. Follow me and I'll show you.'

We tiptoed out to the hall and, making less noise than a mouse on a soft carpet, crept into the back room and walked over to the window. The room was dark, so we could see out easily.

A few small, skinny evergreen trees swayed in the breeze, just over the fence at the end of the garden, on the piece of waste ground that didn't belong to anyone. They looked a bit spooky in the dark.

'It's not exactly a forest,' he said. 'The trees where I come from are so tall you can barely see the tops.'

I could see what he meant. Though at least we wouldn't freeze to death at the back of our garden.

We left the room and went back to the living room and sat down on the sofa. My eyes fell on the tray, on the teapot, on Marco's cup of tea with milk and no sugar.

'I know it's not perfect here,' I said, 'but there's a shed down at the end of the garden. You could sleep there. No one would have to know. And I could bring you tea every day.'

I could see that he liked what I was saying. In
his heart he must have known he would never get
back to his family in the Rockies. And he
definitely wouldn't get Mum's tea there!

'I can sleep in the shed?'

'For as long as you want. No one goes near the shed.'

'Not even your mum?'

'She hates the shed. It reminds her of Dad, because Dad built it. It's a nice shed. All it needs is a bit of cleaning out.'

The piece of land beyond the garden was already a North American forest in my mind's eye.

I began to tell him about the trails we could make through the trees. And the little stream at the far side.

'We could build a bridge across the river.'

'I thought you said it was a stream?'

'A stream in the summer, a fast-flowing river in the winter.'

He tipped the cup and emptied it in one huge gulp.

'I'll stay so,' he said. 'I could do with a nice long rest. And a bit of company.'

'Me, too,' I said.